Noddy and the Magic Bagpipes

HarperCollins *Children's Books*

It was a chilly day in Toyland…

Big-Ears and Noddy were playing a game in
Toadstool House. Noddy was puzzling over his
next move, when Big-Ears wanted a warm rug.
Noddy leaped up. "I'll get it!" he said.

BLARRRRP!

"Agghh!" gasped Noddy. "There's a monster in your cupboard, Big-Ears!"

Big-Ears strode towards the cupboard.

"Ooooh! Be careful, Big-Ears," Noddy warned him. "It sounds very angry."

Big-Ears reached into the cupboard.

BLARRRRP!

Noddy jumped back in horror.

Big-Ears chuckled. "Don't be scared, Noddy," he said. "That's not a monster. That's my bagpipes. I can play music on them. Listen."

Big-Ears took a big, deep breath and blew into the
bagpipes. His fingers danced over the holes and the
bagpipes let out a loud *wagh-wagh-wagh* tune.

"What a wonderful sound!" sighed Noddy,
dreamily. How magical it would be if *he* could
play the bagpipes!

"Will you teach me to play?" Noddy asked.

"It takes a lot of time and practice to play the bagpipes, Noddy," Big-Ears warned.

"But I really want to learn. Please teach me, Big-Ears," Noddy begged.

Big-Ears looked serious. "These are special bagpipes, Noddy," he said. "They need a lot of care. And you must practise. You have to play them every day."

"Yes, yes, I'll do it," agreed Noddy. "I'll work really hard, Big-Ears, I promise."

Big-Ears smiled as they got ready for Noddy's
first lesson.

"Let's start now," whooped Noddy.

"I'll teach you a simple tune," said Big-Ears.
"Then you must practise it every single day.
Understand?"

"Yes, Big-Ears," said Noddy, eagerly. "I'll practise
first thing, every day."

Next morning, Noddy leaped out of bed.
He wrestled the bagpipes into position,
took a big, deep breath and blew.
  BLARRRPP-RRRNNNNN-SSSSSHHH!
  "That didn't sound anything like the tune
Big-Ears played," grumbled Noddy. "I'll try again."
  And he took another big, deep breath.

But just as Noddy was about to blow into
the pipes, he saw his yellow kite leaning against
the wall.

"There's a perfect breeze today. I think I'll
fly my kite," said Noddy, throwing the bagpipes
on to the chair. "I can always practise tomorrow."

Next morning, Noddy was just about to start
practising, when he heard Mr Sparks' voice.

"Hey, Noddy! Do you want to come fishing?"

"Sorry! I'm rather busy," Noddy called down.

Then he saw Mr Sparks' fishing rod.

"I can always practise the bagpipes tomorrow,"
Noddy said to himself.

And again, he dropped them on the chair.

The following morning, Noddy said to himself, "Today, I won't let anything stop me from practising."

And he leaped out of bed and reached for the bagpipes. But the wonderful bagpipes had gone!

Noddy searched everywhere for them.

"Oh dear, Big-Ears *will* be upset!" he cried.

Down at his garage, Mr Sparks was busy working
on a car.

The bagpipes crept up quietly beside him and...
BLARRRP!

"Yahhhhh!" Mr Sparks jumped back and clunked
his head. "What was THAT?" he wondered, looking
up and down the empty street.

In the square, Dinah Doll was putting the last
building block on a tower.

"There," she said, happily. "Now everyone will
notice my stall."

BLARRRP! The cheeky bagpipes gave poor
Dinah such a fright, she tumbled off her ladder.

"Whoaaaahh!" she yelled as she fell in a
shower of blocks.

Dinah Doll and Mr Sparks were telling Mr Plod what had happened, when Noddy ran up to them.

"Mr Plod, there's been a bagpipes robbery!"

"Bagpipes, eh?" said Mr Plod. "I've just heard about a mysterious musical instrument on the loose in Toy Town."

BLARRRP! BLARRRP! BLARRRP!

"Listen!" cried Noddy. "It's the bagpipes."

Just at that moment, there was a clattering sound and Noddy and his friends looked round. But all they saw was a blur of tartan as the bagpipes dashed past.

WHEEEET! Mr Plod blew his whistle.

"Stop in the name of Plod!" he ordered, but the bagpipes took no notice and ran on, whining and wailing.

Mr Plod chased the bagpipes all around the town, trying to grab them. Noddy, Mr Sparks and Dinah watched, amazed.

Nimbly, the bagpipes leaped out of Mr Plod's reach and sped away.

"Oooof," he gasped.

"Looks like Mr Plod needs our help," said Dinah.

But the cheeky bagpipes leaped up at Dinah and
Mr Sparks, and then clattered away as they
tumbled over backwards.

"Ouch!" they both cried.

"Come back here, you!" shouted Noddy.

But the bagpipes took no notice.

Noddy ran round and round after the bagpipes,
until he was dizzy.

"Now where has that pesky thing gone?"
he wondered. BLAARRRP!

Noddy looked up. Perched on a branch were
the bagpipes. He grabbed one of the dangling pipes
and pulled.

"Got you!" he yelled.

Noddy held on tight, but the bagpipes began to grow bigger and bigger.

Suddenly, they let out a loud BLARRP! and took off. They were flying!

"Help! Help!" Noddy shouted, clinging on to the whooshing bagpipes.

As Noddy swooped past, Mr Plod grabbed hold of his feet. But Mr Plod was swept up into the air as well!

"Aghhh!" he gasped.

Then Mr Sparks grabbed on to Mr Plod's legs and Dinah grabbed Mr Sparks' legs.

But the clever bagpipes swooped down under a park bench – and zoomed out the other side without them.

That night, the bagpipes' non-stop wailing kept the whole of Toy Town awake.

Noddy gave up trying to sleep.

"I have to catch those bagpipes," he groaned.

Suddenly, Noddy heard a loud knocking on his door. Perhaps it was the bagpipes? He jumped out of bed.

"Big-Ears!" cried Noddy, as he opened the door.

"You didn't practise, did you?" said Big-Ears, crossly. "I warned you those bagpipes had to be played every day."

"I'm sorry, Big-Ears. I *did* mean to," Noddy said sadly.

He looked so upset that Big-Ears sighed, "Don't worry, Noddy. I just get grumpy when I'm tired."

"But why are the bagpipes running around
screeching?" asked Noddy. "And keeping us all
awake?"

"Magic," explained Big-Ears. "These bagpipes get
restless if they're not played every day. They just
want to make music – but they need help...
which gives me an idea, Noddy!"

"A-one, a-two, a-three," said Big-Ears to his brand new band in Toy Town park.

BUZZ-BUZZ-BUZZ went Dinah on the kazoo.

WHEET-WHEET went Mr Plod on his whistle.

BOOM-BOOM went Mr Sparks on an oil drum.

And Noddy sang:

> *The best thing about this simple song*
> *Is that anyone can play along...*

The bagpipes watched the band. Then they leaped on to Noddy's chair.

Scooping them on to his lap, Noddy took a big, deep breath and blew. *Wagh-wagh-wagh…*

The bagpipes were happy now that they were making music in a real band.

And Noddy played every note perfectly.

"Wonderful!" said Big-Ears. "Our music has tamed the bagpipes!"

"But I think you ought to give them back to Big-Ears for safe-keeping, Noddy," said Mr Sparks.

"Yes," said Noddy. "You'd better have the bagpipes, Big-Ears. I might not practise every day!"

"OK, Noddy," said Big-Ears, smiling. "But first, let's play our tune just one more time."

"Right!" said Noddy, and took a big, deep breath.
    And the new Toy Town band gave one last
wonderful performance.

The best thing about this simple song
Is that anyone can play along.
Listen to the tune, and feel the beat,
Then clap your hands and stamp your feet!

This edition produced for The Book People Ltd,
Hall Wood Avenue, Haydock, St Helens, WA11 9UL
First published in Great Britain by HarperCollins Publishers Ltd in 2003

1

This edition published by HarperCollins Children's Books
HarperCollins Children's Books is a division of HarperCollins Publishers Ltd.

ISBN: 978 0 00 783068 8

Visit our website at: www.harpercollinschildrensbooks.co.uk

Printed and bound by South China Printing Co. Ltd